S0-BYK-102

DEEP DOWN UNDERGROUND

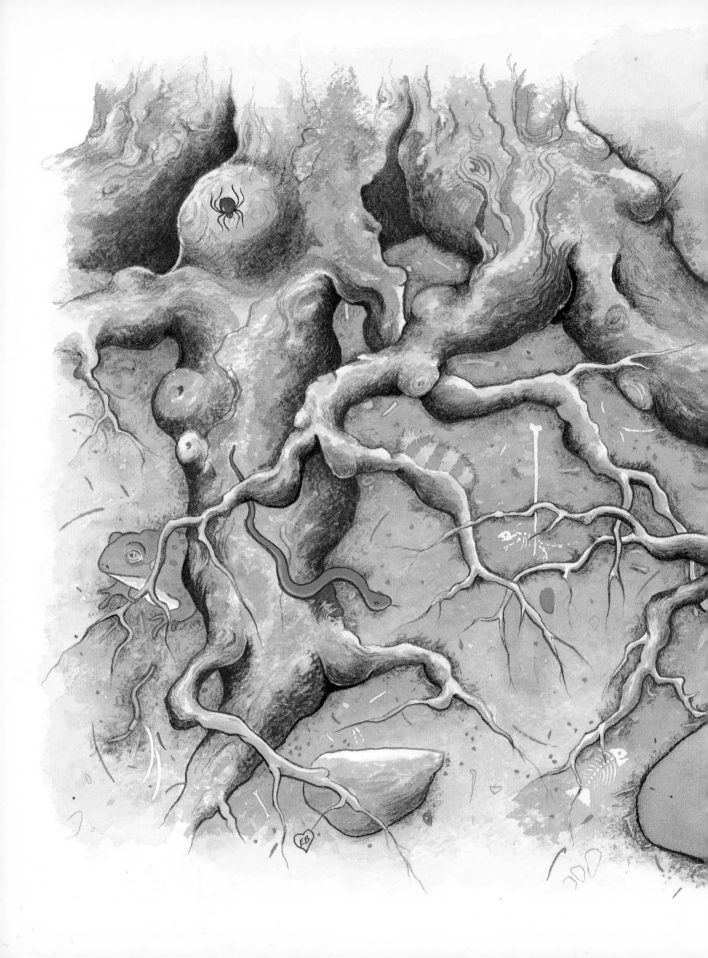

DEEP DOWN UNDERGROUND

by Olivier Dunrea

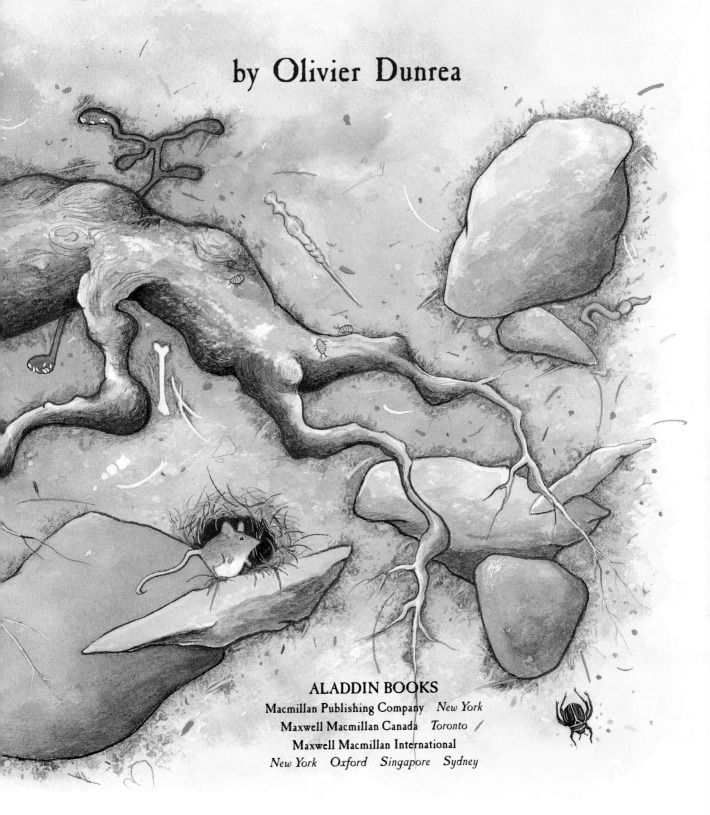

ALADDIN BOOKS
Macmillan Publishing Company   *New York*
Maxwell Macmillan Canada   *Toronto*
Maxwell Macmillan International
New York   Oxford   Singapore   Sydney

First Aladdin Books edition 1993. Copyright © 1989 by Olivier Dunrea. All rights reserved. No part of this book may be reproduced or transmitted in any form or by any means, electronic or mechanical, including photocopying, recording, or by any information storage and retrieval system, without permission in writing from the Publisher. Aladdin Books, Macmillan Publishing Company, 866 Third Avenue, New York, NY 10022. Maxwell Macmillan Canada, Inc., 1200 Eglinton Avenue East, Suite 200, Don Mills, Ontario M3C 3N1. Macmillan Publishing Company is part of the Maxwell Communication Group of Companies. Printed in Singapore.
10 9 8 7 6 5 4 3 2 1

The text of this book is set in 16 point Caslon Antique. The illustrations are rendered in pen-and-ink and watercolor. A hardcover edition of *Deep Down Underground* is available from Macmillan Publishing Company.

Library of Congress Cataloging–in–Publication Data
Dunrea, Olivier.
    Deep down underground / by Olivier Dunrea.—1st Aladdin Books ed.
      p.   cm.
    Summary: Animals present the numbers from one to ten, as earthworms, toads, ants, and others march and burrow, scurry and scooch deep down underground.
    ISBN 0-689-71756-3
    [1. Animals—Fiction.   2. Counting.]   I. Title.
  [PZ7.D922De 1993]
  [E]—dc20   92-45273

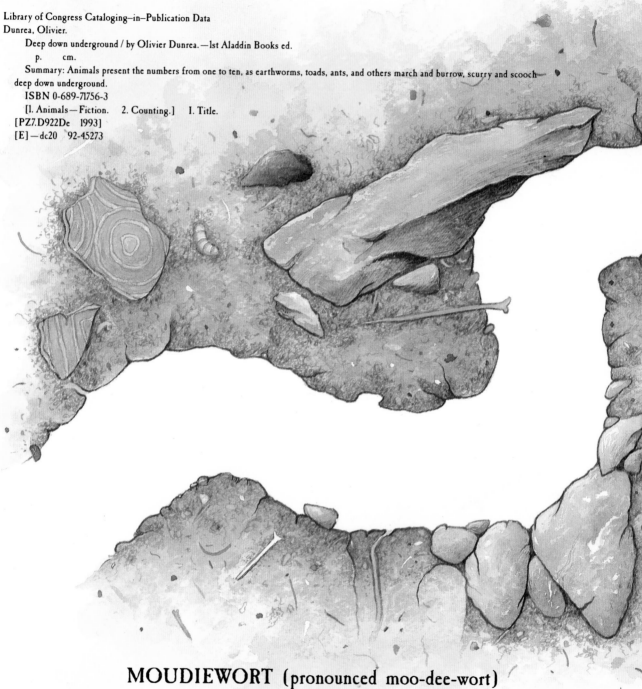

MOUDIEWORT (pronounced moo-dee-wort)
is a Scottish word for mole.

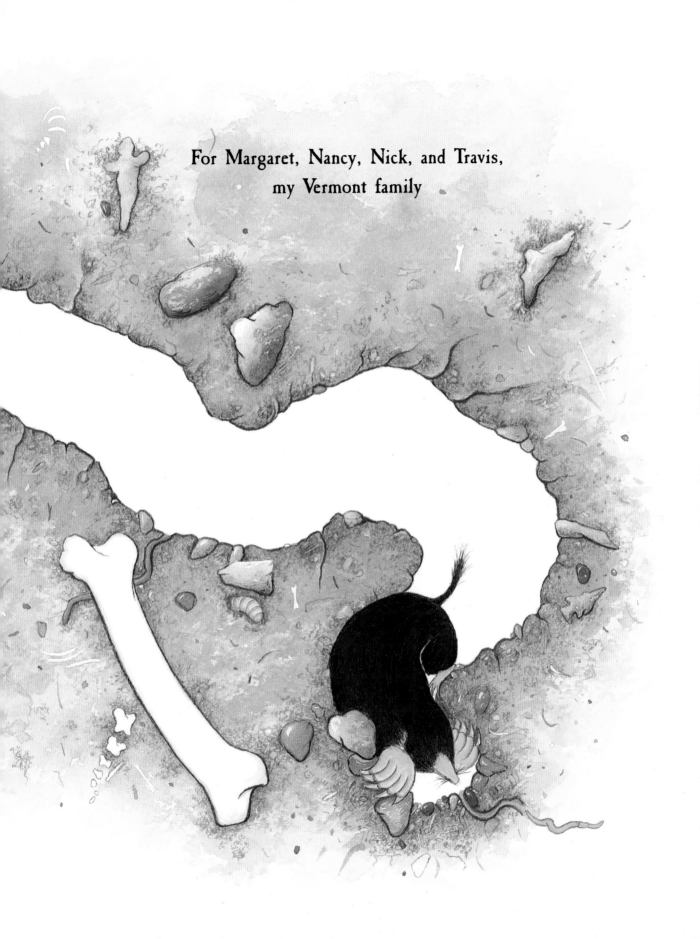

For Margaret, Nancy, Nick, and Travis,
my Vermont family

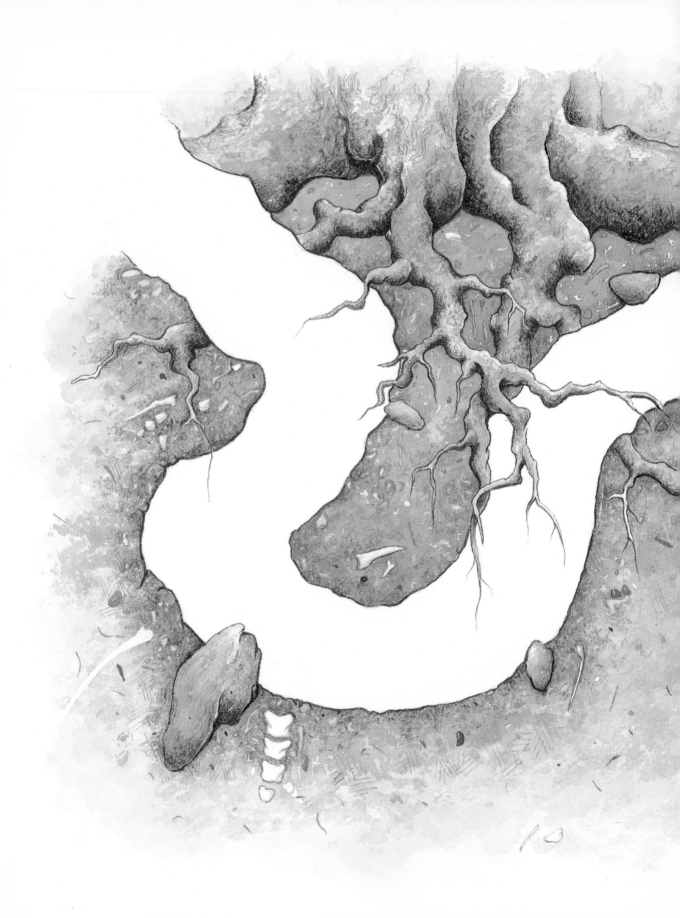

Deep down underground
l wee moudiewort digs and digs
deep down underground.

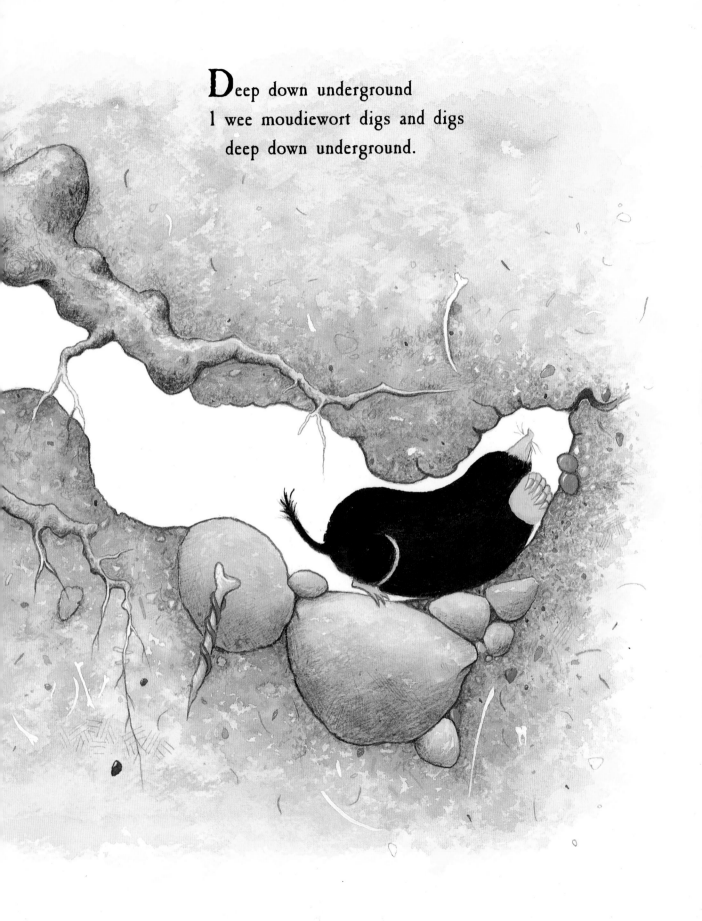

2 pink earthworms wriggle and wrangle when they hear
1 wee moudiewort digging, digging
     deep down underground.

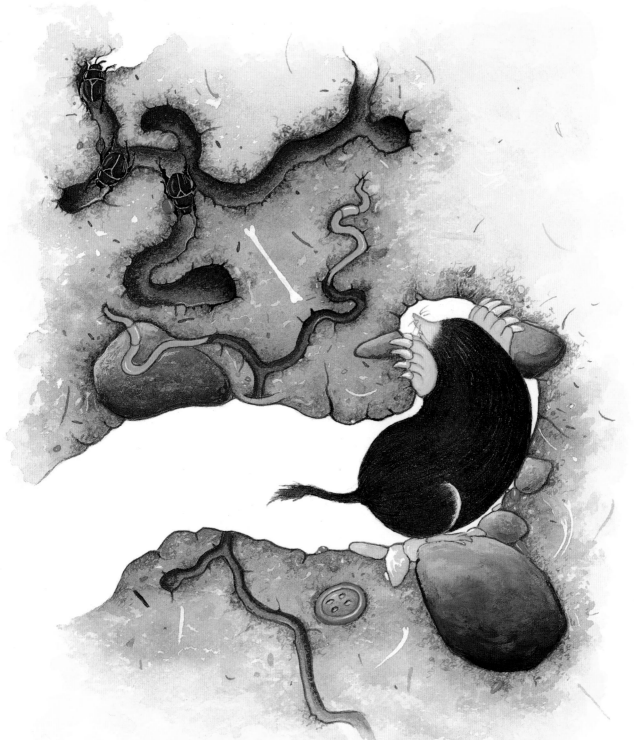

3 big black beetles scurry and scamper when they hear
2 pink earthworms wriggle and wrangle when they hear
1 wee moudiewort digging, digging
 deep down underground.

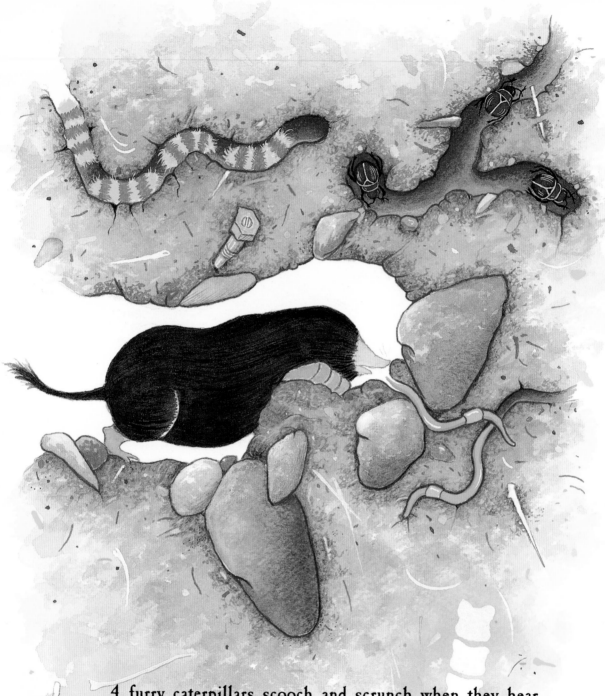

4 furry caterpillars scooch and scrunch when they hear
3 big black beetles scurry and scamper when they hear
2 pink earthworms wriggle and wrangle when they hear
1 wee moudiewort digging, digging
  deep down underground.

5 fat spiders dance and prance when they hear
4 furry caterpillars scooch and scrunch when they hear
3 big black beetles scurry and scamper when they hear
2 pink earthworms wriggle and wrangle when they hear
1 wee moudiewort digging, digging
   deep down underground.

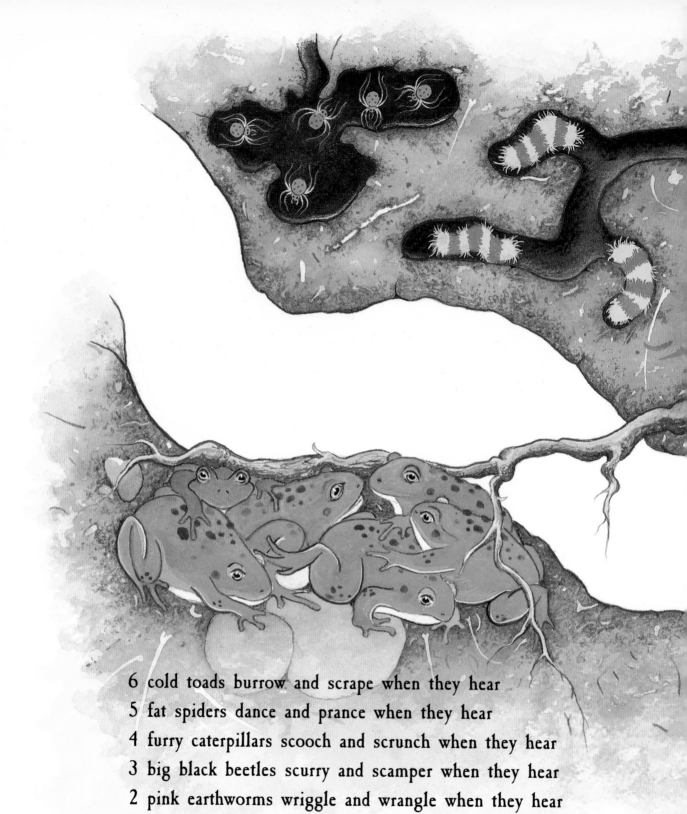

6 cold toads burrow and scrape when they hear
5 fat spiders dance and prance when they hear
4 furry caterpillars scooch and scrunch when they hear
3 big black beetles scurry and scamper when they hear
2 pink earthworms wriggle and wrangle when they hear
1 wee moudiewort digging, digging
   deep down underground.

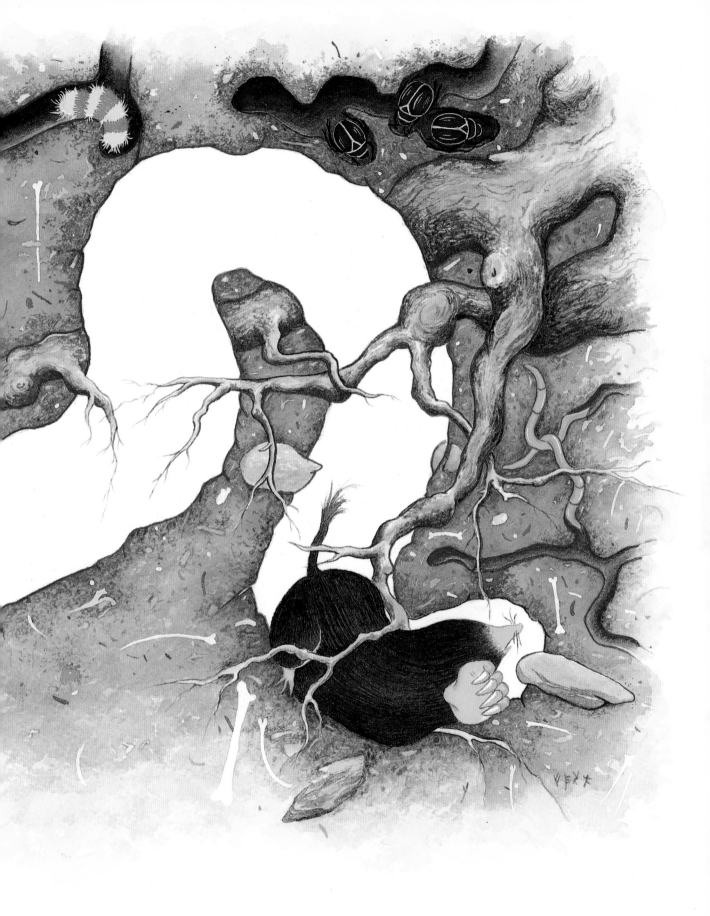

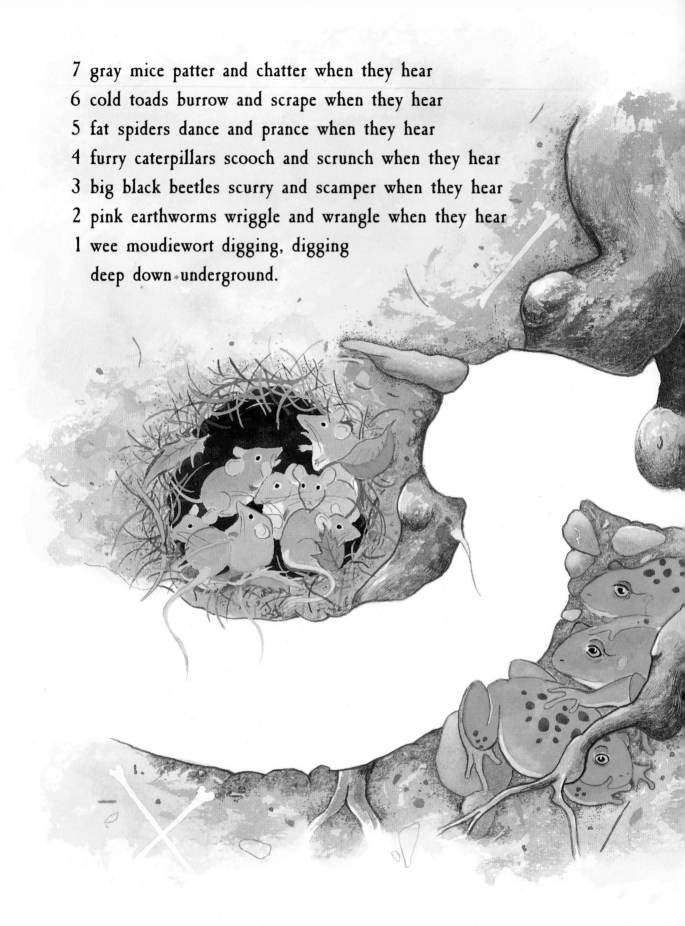

7 gray mice patter and chatter when they hear
6 cold toads burrow and scrape when they hear
5 fat spiders dance and prance when they hear
4 furry caterpillars scooch and scrunch when they hear
3 big black beetles scurry and scamper when they hear
2 pink earthworms wriggle and wrangle when they hear
1 wee moudiewort digging, digging
   deep down underground.

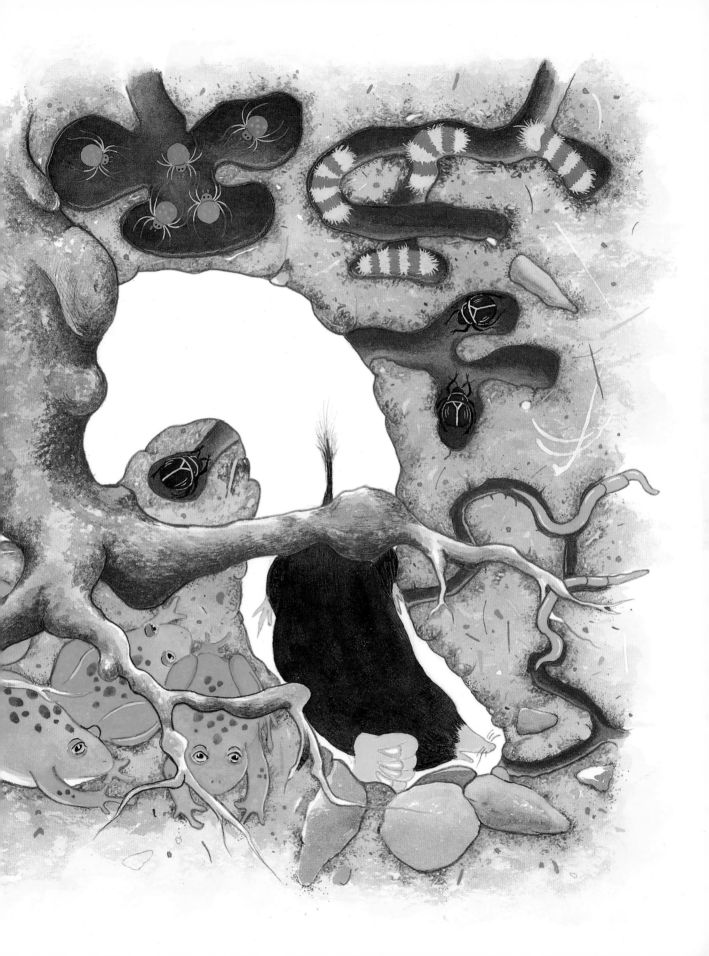

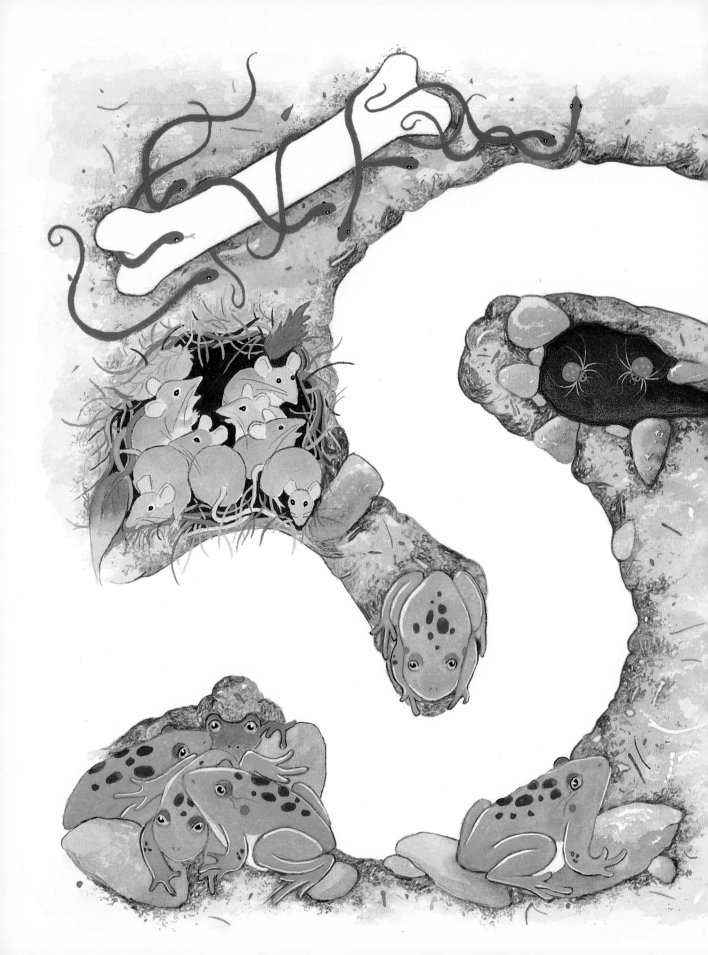

8 green garter snakes slide and glide when they hear
7 gray mice patter and chatter when they hear
6 cold toads burrow and scrape when they hear
5 fat spiders dance and prance when they hear
4 furry caterpillars scooch and scrunch when they hear
3 big black beetles scurry and scamper when they hear
2 pink earthworms wriggle and wrangle when they hear
1 wee moudiewort digging, digging
   deep down underground.

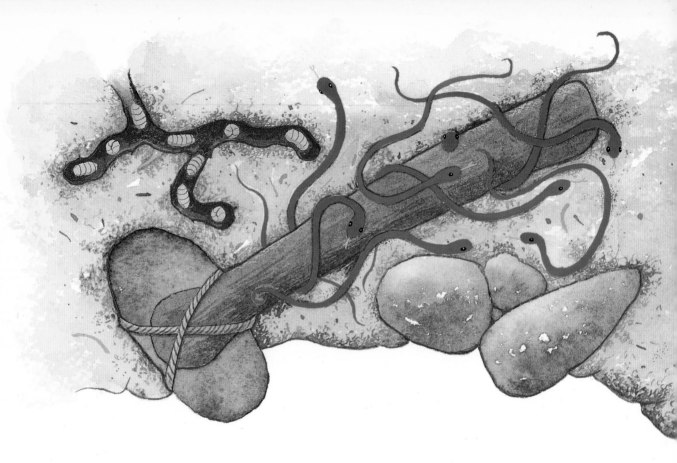

9 armored sow bugs run and roll when they hear
8 green garter snakes slide and glide when they hear
7 gray mice patter and chatter when they hear
6 cold toads burrow and scrape when they hear
5 fat spiders dance and prance when they hear
4 furry caterpillars scooch and scrunch when they hear
3 big black beetles scurry and scamper when they hear
2 pink earthworms wriggle and wrangle when they hear
1 wee moudiewort digging, digging
    deep down underground.

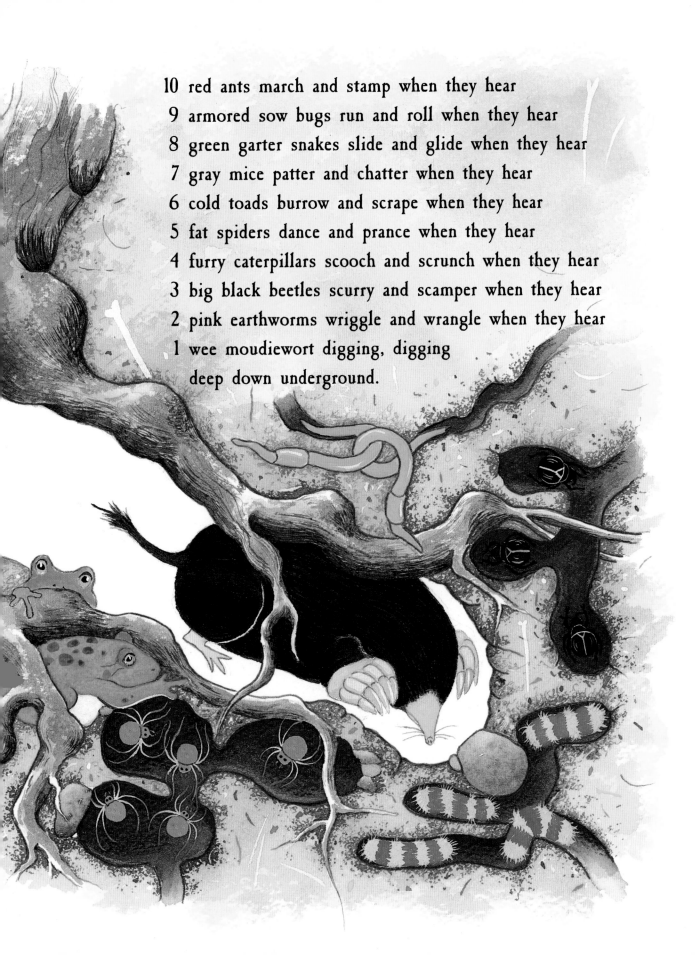

10 red ants march and stamp when they hear
9 armored sow bugs run and roll when they hear
8 green garter snakes slide and glide when they hear
7 gray mice patter and chatter when they hear
6 cold toads burrow and scrape when they hear
5 fat spiders dance and prance when they hear
4 furry caterpillars scooch and scrunch when they hear
3 big black beetles scurry and scamper when they hear
2 pink earthworms wriggle and wrangle when they hear
1 wee moudiewort digging, digging
deep down underground.

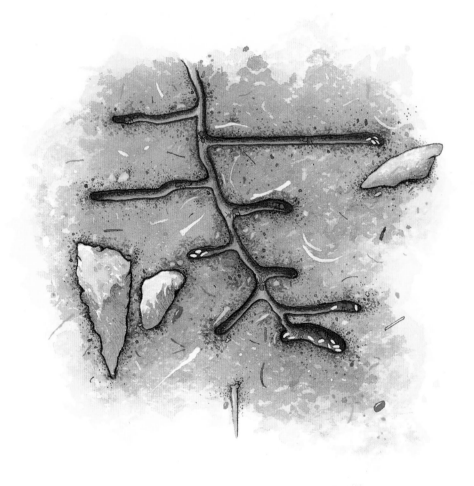

Then... 10 red ants STOP marching and stamping when they hear

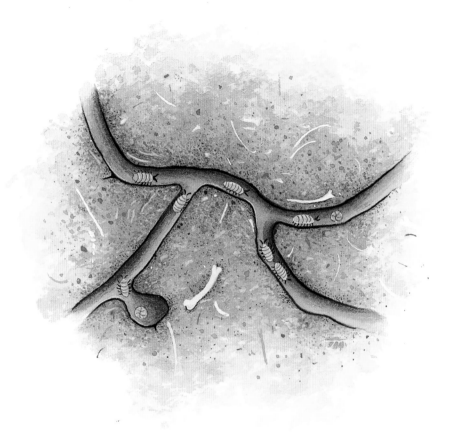

9 armored sow bugs STOP running and rolling when they hear

8 green garter snakes **STOP** sliding and gliding when they hear

7 gray mice **STOP** pattering and chattering when they hear

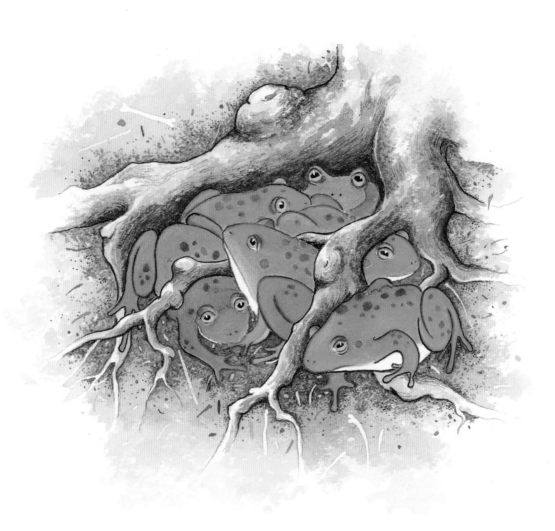

6 cold toads **STOP** burrowing and scraping when they hear

5 fat spiders STOP dancing and prancing when they hear

4 furry caterpillars STOP scooching and scrunching when they hear

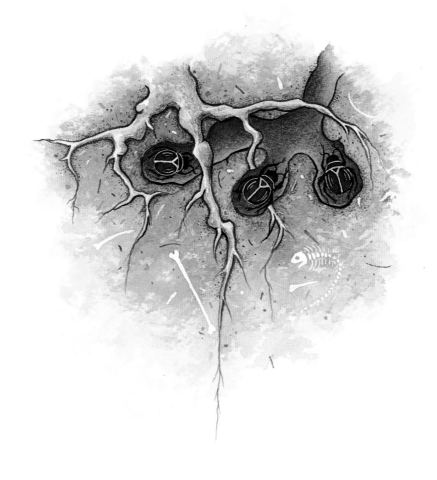

3 big black beetles STOP scurrying and scampering when they hear

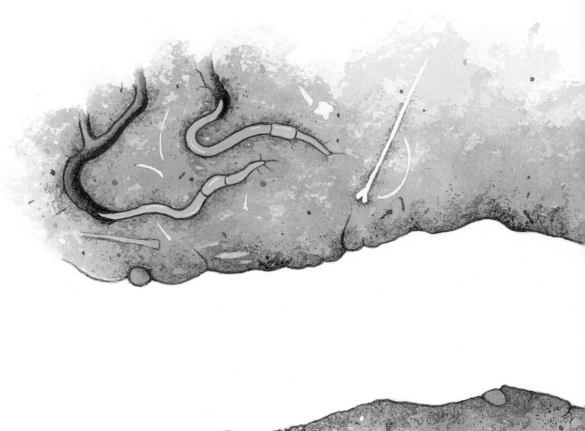

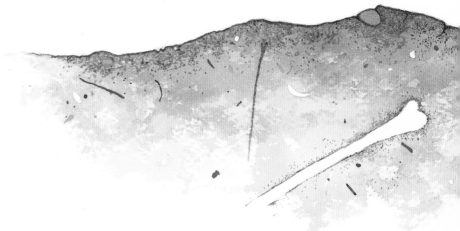

2 pink earthworms STOP wriggling and wrangling when they hear

1 wee moudiewort SNEEZE!
deep down underground.